Poetry and Short Stories

By

Sharon Brummer

Author: Sharon Brummer
Book cover: Heleen Malherbe
Set in Calibri 12 pt

First Edition 2019

Copyright © Sharon Brummer
ISBN 9798614451417

Published and printed by Malherbe Publishers

WITH NARRATION DESCRIBING THE
PERSONAL EMOTION, BE IT FUNNY OR SAD,
BEHIND EACH GROUP OF POEMS.

Index:

MY INHERENT LOVE FOR WRITING.

I've always wanted to write. At school I would write plays, poems, and short stories. Fortunately I had Principals who also loved writing. They were my first mentors and inspiration in picking up my pen.

After my busy career of 30 years with an international electronics company, I decided to start writing full time. My first two adult novels were published, and then three children's books – ages 5-10. Each book contains three stories on the same little boy. In between I started writing poems. Thus this book of poetry.

For the love of writing

Be it a quill or a pen
Write I shall
Be the mountains laden with wise men
Inspired I shall be
Be the fields sprinkled with color
Write my stories I shall

Be the surface papyrus scroll or paper
Write I shall
Time is of no consequence, nor greater
Make haste, write on
Stain my hands dear ink
Of plots I shall think

Move little ball pen, quick and sure
Interpret my thoughts I shall
Highlight my love for writing so pure
The written word I hunger for
Poetry, fiction, so many books
These are my hooks

Write, the purpose of my life
Blood characters I conjure
No matter the strain and strife
Dream on shall I
In the dead of the night
I shall write

Escapism by book

Quiet, peaceful evening
Lost in chapters, fire crackling
Touch of paper so soothing
Discovered in ancient civilizations
Impossible feats of dramatic illusions
Carefully crafted compositions

Books – the only tangible object
Transports you to a magical planet
Escape from this world
Magic in my lap – legends lured
Conjuring up wizard and hero
My cup runneth over

Woven tapestry of thought
Pirates, Merlin, Mary Poppins – creativity onslaught
Characters on cue alike puppets
Sound the trumpets
Bound by a spine
Spun and multiplied by a line

Colored words

Colors clash, burn, swirl and split
Torn apart in a melting pit
Raging energy and danger
Quench power of anger
Serenity hope with positivity
Brain filled with creativity
Find the words of my happiness

Words filled with sunshine
Purification war of mine
Fuel joy conflicting fire
Burning heart ceasefire
Violence grips the hand
Hold gentle each round

Evolve rich color enlightenment
Coat my words with judgment
Good and evil – Find my colored words

THE GOOD OLD DAYS

At certain times of your life, you wish you could turn the clock back, to be young again. To reenact precious memories of childhood. To sit on a bench with your favorite people who have sadly passed on. I have so much to tell them, although I speak to them in my dreams.

The next poem was written on one of those nostalgic days.

I want to be young again

I want
to splash in the rain gutters
to be carried on my father's shoulders
to run in the pouring rain
I want to be young again

I want
to play marbles at school break
excitement which makes me shake
speed recklessly on my bicycle
to listen to upbeat music, not classical

I want
to hear my mother calling me
no responsibility
to play in the streets with my friends
to carve my name in wood with my pens

I want
dirt on my dress
my dolls to caress
to watch the clouds for hours
lounging on a bed of flowers

I want
to be young again
to love the rainbow stain
I want to read books, pretending I'm the writer
to write without being older, just wiser

I want to be young again
Forever young

THE CORPORATE WORLD

My corporate career was exciting and challenging. My determination, work ethic and honesty guided my career whilst working for an international electronic corporate company. Initially I was one of the few female managers. Fortunately additional opportunities for the female were afforded as the years progressed.

Looking back on my career, I think my colleagues will agree with the sentiments expressed in the poem below.

Grace versus scorn

I walk in my own footsteps
I stride strong and true
I'll meet anyone toe to toe, on cue

Do not try to intimidate me
Do not try to bully me
Do not dare abuse me

My grandmother survived wars
My grandmother read her husband's their last rites
My grandmother campaigned for women's rights

I learnt to fight manipulation with scorn
before my attribute of grace was born
Now my head with grace adorn

My strongest ally was honesty
Work ethic my best policy
Success and pride I claim constantly

The corporate jungle

The corporate jungle
No matter your title
Only the fittest survive
Colleagues' honesty you surmise.
Deadlines to meet
Develop your inner athlete

The traffic relentless
The taxi drivers heartless
Horns blaring
Tempers flaring
Still to arrive at the office
Still to dance to political lyric

Office environment mimics traffic
Dramatic not dynamic
Ego's relentless
Inapt executors clueless
Blowing their own horn
Tempers flaring in scorn

Budget forecast meeting
Achievements oh so fleeting
Do or die
Unless you have an irresistible smile
My graph climbs high and proud
Strange no one bowed
Stab in your back!

Who was that?
Coward show yourself
Politically correct – herself or himself
Adapt to change
Improve your aim at the firing range

Important tools in your kit
Perfume – to overpower the smell of a hypocrite
Mouth guard – pure grit
Comfortable shoes – stand your ground
Red lipstick – power compound
Sense of humor – to agree with boss newly crowned

THE INEVITABILITY OF IMMIGRATION

With my children and grandsons living in Australia I find myself torn. Happy that they are safe but selfishly sad that my husband and I are not there to share their daily life. Especially sad that we are not there to witness our grandsons growing up. Thank goodness we were blessed to experience a wonderful childhood with our sons and build up an unbreakable bond. We know this bond will continue with our grandsons.

My sisters are both also in Australia. When we see each other, time is but a word. The bond that sisters share is fortunately not affected by distance.

Always there

Kiss the toes, the little hands
Reaching out, exploring his face
While he deciphers the space
Your baby finds his voice
Mimic his sounds, and rejoice
No matter what, Mom's always there
Always there to care
To satisfy his hunger
To rock him in slumber
To sooth away his tears

Kiss the grubby hands
Playing in the sand
Mom's gentle command
Gleefully tickling his stomach
Laughing as he fills his bucket
Standing on squat unsteady legs
Entrenched in the sand like pegs
Knowing that she will catch
Toddlers pace she will match
Always there to lift him high

Kiss the hands – larger than yours
You taught him to open doors
Place your head against a broad chest
Both so blessed
He ruffles your hair
With so much care
Together so wise
That bond unbreakable
'Mom I still need you' - our love unmistakable

Faraway continent

Rise luminous orange glow
Hear the soft cooing of the crow
Sprinkle gold dust over my piece of earth
New resplendent day give birth

Sadly I experience a new day
Whilst my children's day fades away
Eight hours difference on a faraway continent
They left with sadness albeit confident

Run in the dew wet grass
Drink from deceptive lakes mimicking glass
Smell the fresh new dawn
Touch the moist green lawn

Sadly I run, smell, and touch dawn alone
Heavy heart do not moan
Eight hours difference on a faraway continent
Brings safety and peace on their slice of planet

Sandy path reach out to the heavens
Keep my children safe in their havens
Another new day of longing
From one continent to another dawning

Immigration called my family

From one beautiful country to a faraway harmony
I feel, they feel, our hearts beat as one in purity
Cruel sea you cannot separate our hearts in honesty

15

Mastering the art of being far away

Chubby Rosy cheeks
Age – only four weeks
Bow shaped perfect lips
More perfect than the moon eclipse
Big hungry eyes
Watched over by eyes so wise
Trying to master the art of movement

Splashing gleefully in the bath
Heart of granny knows no wrath
Accusing finger complete with pout
Don't mess with this bean sprout
Running – falling – crocodile tears
These are granny's heirs
Trying to master the art of cuteness

Scoring goals – what a shot!
Such magic invaluable - not to be bought
Cycling down the treacherous hill
Granny needs a worry pill
Swimming – diving – utmost confidence
Learning process – now autonomous
Trying to master the art of perfection

Granny blowing kisses
Granny's jokes have grandchildren in stiches
Granny mimics the pointed finger
Granny would love to linger
Granny remembers heartbreak at having to return
home
Granny all alone – shaking hands write this poem
Granny trying to master the art of being so far away

Photographs

In my heart I hold a photo album
All my memories that hold me ransom
Survival memories I cannot live without
The roots of my life devout

Each photograph is a mirror
of my love and emotions
A mirror of life's devotions
As the sea constantly gives to the seagulls – the
giver

Nostalgia brings tears sometimes
Sometimes pure happiness
Beloved faces remembered with tenderness
As the sun remembers to highlight our days
oftentimes

I see our children laughing
I see a young me loving
Me nurturing
The tree of life

I see my mother
dancing with my children
Precious metamorphosis to butterflies
Startling colors, darting flight across the skies

I see and hear my father whistling
Tears mist my vision
All these memories I envision
In the warmth of the wind, him singing

I see my husband playing ball
with our boys
Together – so disarming with happy noise
Rock solid as the mountain – no fall

Should my memories ever fade
remind me of the photos I hold
in my heart – more valuable than gold
More precious than jade

Photographs reflect my soul
I shall hold them forever
and ever – forget never
As long as earth revolves

Forever and after
I have a photograph of you
Remember the me you knew
On earth or in heaven

The middle seat

Excited I buckle up
The middle seat – what bad luck
Australia here I come!
Excitement turns to nausea – face glum
Each turn to the left
Leaves my sense of smell bereft

Flanked by two distinct characters
The writer in me labels them abusers
One nerd complete with dirty nails and hair
His sour smell drifting in the air
My nose twitches, wishing for a peg
My neck disabled – poised to the right – a wreck

I examine the character on my right
This is going to be a long night
She's definitely a mass murderer
In fact, me thinks, together they the torturer
A stoic, pasty face, eyes cunning
Hannibal Lecter - her mouth constantly sucking

Scrambling for my pen and paper
I start my new book – armed with fear and anger
Murdering as many victims as possible
In the first chapter – torture no obstacle
The weapons they use treacherous
The games their play dangerous
Fourteen hours not long enough

Reluctantly alighting from the plane is tough
I need to finish the murder plot
Although my nose and neck are shot
I bid both a hesitant farewell
Admitting I'm under their spell

Rushing for my connecting flight
Wagga Wagga – what a sight
Victims aplenty
I've accomplished my bounty
In the freezing cold, I choose a bench
My thirst for victims will not quench.

A Child's happiness

A child's laughter holds the key
A child's smile melts the heart
A child's hand holds the secret
The key to happiness

A child's mischievous freckle
A child's footprint so special
A child's joyful eyes
The eyes of innocence

A child's heart in you believes
A child's trust lay in your heart
A child's head rests in your beliefs
The belief is sacred

A child will seek the key to happiness
A child will see the shine in your eyes
A child is blessings aplenty
Hold the child tightly

Hope

Not tangible
Not measurable

Purely a heartfelt wish
Purely a prop to nourish

Silently a prayer
Silently bearing despair

A mother's hope
A mother's love and prayer

Not for herself
Not for ears deaf

Hear my plea
Answer me

Grant me the key
To my children's happiness and safety

The bond of sisters

Sisters remember I am the oldest
Not always the coolest
Also not the craziest
Perhaps the most spontaneous

Sisters I was the mother while mom was working
I was supposed to be playing and learning
but no, I had to drag the two of you around
to movies, shops, and then homeward bound

Now we live on different continents
Despite our few arguments
we have an unbreakable bond
which forever will be and beyond

Sisters I confess to stealing
your socks instead of me washing
mine, but then you stole my makeup
as you played dress up

We have a sense of humor
A line we just have to murmur
Only we understand the laughter
Whenever we get together to chatter

Sisters no one knows our past
as we do – what a contrast
our life is now – our trials
and tribulations are now in our life profiles

Sisters, beloved ones lost we miss
Good memories we reminisce
Survival we've been taught
This life we have fought

Sisters, with tears and laughter
here's to many more forever after

AFRICA – MY HEART – COASTAL BEAUTY

I've been fortunate enough to travel extensively, both in my career and on holidays with my family. I'm always happy to return to South Africa though. This country has a vibe and luster never experienced in any other country.

I grew up in the city however I now live in a beautiful coastal town. How fortunate are we. The seasons each offer their own beauty and fingerprint. Dotted around Mossel Bay are quaint Antique shops offering treasures of yesteryear.

If only we could eradicate the crime and corruption in our amazing country, South Africa would be the perfect paradise.

Africa – where my heart and soul roam

I've travelled the globe extensively
Reveling in foreign sights and sounds endlessly

Drinking Aqua from the Trevi Fountain
By Funicular from Lake Lucerne to the mountain

Mind capturing the castles down the Rhine River
Drifting on Lake Wakatipu, flat as a mirror

Spying guards at Buckingham Palace
Chandeliers at Palace Versailles armed with chalice
Only meeting the landlords at Madam Tussauds

Opera sung on a Gondola through Venice waters
Instantly one of the aspiring authors

Up, up, up, to the Eiffel Tower
Breathtaking scene below to scour
Thank goodness not the leaning Tower of Pisa

Twinkle, twinkle, little stars of Hong Kong
As we cross on the ferry at the sound of the gong

Moulin Rouge – dancing and drinking champagne
As opposed to meditation at the Thailand temples
reign

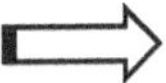

Waffles and buckets of mussels
In the Grand Palace of Brussels

Tears at the piano at Graceland
Singing at the Sun Studios' bandstand

Dancing in the streets of New Orleans
Fairytale in Heidelberg – what an audience

Yangtze River – hide your dark secrets
Foretell phantom stories, I feel your bleakness

Ultimately my heart cries out for Africa
Not for Asia, Europe, Australasia or America

I long for the crushing waves of The Wilderness
The vineyards of the Cape, Table Mountain so
rigorous

I long for the smells of Fynbos and Rooibos
The Skeleton Coast where shipwrecks crisscross

I long for the expanse of the Kruger Park
The thunderous Victoria falls as a Landmark

I long for Africa – My home
Where my heart and soul roam

Load shedding

The dark is eerie and still
Unfamiliar noises
Flickering candles burns
Shadows climb the walls
Unfamiliar surroundings
Nervous fidgeting hands
Wringing out the hours
Crazy tumbling thoughts
No knocks on unwelcome doors
Just creaking old floors

Silence fights the darkness
No coffee to quell the nervousness
Walls close in on peacefulness
Children to sleep – no playfulness
Too dangerous for pureness

Finally solace of my bed whites
No need to turn out the lights
The Electricity Supply Commission has already
blackened out
 Our Bill of Rights

Humankind

Dawn breaks
New beginnings
Past snowflakes
New winnings

Mountains divided
Painted color
Shadows provided
Man scholar

Be kind
New day
Leave behind
Grey decay

You, me
Be free
Be kind
Humankind

Death from suburban war

Thoughts tumble in my head
Head hurts – torment fed
Noise bouncing off walls – disturbs my thoughts
Television too loud – stomach knots
Wash machine tumbling round and round
Tears smarting – vision drowned
Pounding on the bedroom door
Save me from this suburban war
When will this torture stop?

Too much to bear this evil suburban strife
This murderous chaotic life
Dancing on the table
No longer is the mind stable
Save me from myself
Drowning in mundane trials – stress on an empty
shelf
Salvation from my thoughts
To kill me – there are plots
When will they come for my useless body?

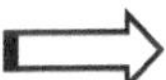

Too late to rescue my soul
Malevolence on cue
Too late to save me
Suburban war has uprooted my life tree
I die with glee
No longer do I plea
Please bury me away from the noise
Bury me away from suburban joys
Bury me in the quiet of a valley, amidst tall aloes

Color of life

Purple dominant – woe is me
Blue skies – press down on me
Yellow halo aura – happy me
Black tornado of life – turn me
Pink cosmos – pretty me
Green fields – run with me
Red tainted blood – flows in me

Life's twists and turns
Body aches and churns
Luck and heartache returns
Spirits' soars and learns

Hold my hand – woe is me
Hero to Villain – fight for me
Rich to poor – feed me
Visual to reality – see me

Me – see me color of life

The suburban mask

I hide behind a lonely suburban mask
I hide behind a robotic smile
I hide behind a false pose
I hide my heartache – no one knows

I paint my face white
Hide as though its night
I paint my lips ruby red
Heavy my heart as lead
I place make-up on my face
I'm frail as old lace

I hide behind a laughing clown
I hide behind the suburban town
I hide behind the vortex of life
No one knows my strife

Shifting seas

The landscape painted to perfection
Brushstrokes by The Painter on reflection
Greys, browns, greens of every hue
Scattered on cue

Up hills, down valleys, wildflowers sprinkled
Flanked by the coastline so wrinkled
Turquoise blue waves tease the shoreline
Polish black rocks to shine

Hungry Seagulls scavenge for food
Dolphins surface, then disappear in playful mood
Sunrays spread glitter over the glistening sea
Spread so vast and free

Sunset brings a new Moon
Turbulent grey seas spew a new tune
Cumulus clouds frown down
As mist hides the colors of the town

Crashing greedy swirls hurl shells
No carefree Dolphins here dwells
Fisherman abandon their fortunate claim
Contortionist waves their stock reclaim

Ships feel the full force of the mighty ocean
The perilous waters pack a poisonous potion

Wind co-ordinates with deafening noise
Inside innocent girls and boys

Winter in Mossel Bay

Birds interrupt sleeping patterns
That mirror – my hair does not flatter
Cold air creeps inside slippers
Hot showers alleviate the bitters
Hope the waters on!

Sun plays hide and seek
Jerseys on and off – the entire week
Heavens open – three drops of rain
A rainstorm in feign
Husband complains – hosepipe in hand

Wind suddenly whips at branches
Slams doors – dogs take their chances
Sea and sky change color
In unison – waves pummel trawler
'Come back to shore – complain wives'

Squawk the Seagulls
Soaring with the Fish Eagles
Use the wind to take them home
Leave behind the angry foam
No complaints – all huddled up for the winter night.

Fields of wheat

The mountains, adorned with snow peaks
cradle the precious field
to safeguard the yield

These fields are my humble home
caught in the cycle of seasons
caught in the cycle of my feelings

Inspire my emotions
as they inspired Vincent van Gogh
Symbolic as the rise of dough

I look to the blessed sun
to the cumulus clouds darkening
Gentle raindrops perfect for harvesting

The people we will feed
The wheat we will harvest
The task of harness

Stand proud tall wheat
Green in the early cycle
Stages professed in our bible

We have no strife in the sacrifice

Nor pretense at modesty
Our knowledge in botany

Proud eyes behold the yield
Our task complete
No small feat

Come winter we start the process again
And again, and again
Cycle of the food chain

How to combat winter

Boots, jerseys and coats
A season without antidotes
Heaters, closed doors, fireplaces
All with flushed faces
Fluffy blankets, sheepskin slippers
Wrapped up warm while the wind whispers
Gloves, scarfs, ears encased in beanies
Definitely no season for bikinis

Red wine, sherry, hot chocolates
I've bankrupt my pockets
Hot Brandy desert with custard
Now I'm totally flustered
Soup, stews, goulash
There goes my diet awash
Many cups of hot tea
For the entire household and me

Whirling winds, icy air
Flyaway hair
Grey skies, dark seas
No surfers in the breeze
Swaying trees, littered leaves
Streets covered in ice, eyes deceives
Barren branches grotesque in posture
Reaching out to torture

I long for a summer day
For the sun to caress my face
I want to run in the warm sea spray
Winter give up your race
Give summer a chance to embrace
We can now walk with grace
No longer bent over and gaunt
Out and about to the new salad restaurant

Autumn leaves

An array of color shed
Heaped on the ground
Nature with color embed
 It's Autumn

Wind whips at the trees
Small and large alike
With absolute ease
It's Autumn

Floating in the air
Leaves caught in the beaks of birds
With so much care
It's Autumn

Crunched by passersby
Dried out colored leaves
Complimentary to the eye
It's Autumn

Amongst the fallen leaves play Squirrels
Hide and Seek
Jumping over heaped hurdles
It's Autumn

Springtime

Since young I yearn for spring
Year after year I shake off winter
Spritely birds too shake off the cold and sing
Fat worms in fresh earthy soil for dinner

Apricot and Peach trees blossom
Sprinkling an array of colored petals
Take to your writing scholar
Whilst spring awakens and settles

Flowers of every hue
Sprout stout stems toward the sky
White petals dipped in blue
A feast for the starved eye

Cherry buds burst
Under the umbrella of their tree
White fluffy blossoms dispersed
Into the wind – light and free

Pop the champagne
It's picnic time
Never a time to complain
A time for rejuvenation – springtime

Summertime theme

Surf boards color the waves
Bronze bodies adorn the beach
Tourists are here in droves
Children and seagulls screech

Bare legs, skimpy dresses
No more indoor messes
Everyone is outside
Enjoying activities such as the wet slide

Delicious meat on a barbeque
Summer salads on cue
Chocolate Chip and Mint ice-cream
So many flavors of which to dream

In summery shades Hydrangea
Our national flower – Protea
Soft Dahlias and Poppies
White scented St Joseph Lilies

This is summertime.

Daisy

Petals formed to perfection
Cause of much affection
Colorful layers a reflection
Mimic the rainbow

Yellow – Innocence and Purity
Pink – Love and Beauty
Orange – New Beginnings and Fertility
Unique you are

Sun you crave anew
Summer day pursue
Flower head full of dew
Go away, then come back again

Crevasses crack to reveal
Trees hug where we kneel
Ceramic Pots to great appeal
Your habitat

Rosette, ovate or smooth
Fountain of youth
Common, Barberton or English – soul to sooth
Just a name, just a flower

Dazzle my senses – Dazzle my eyes – Daisy

Antique treasures

Antique treasure coves
Cherish the porcelain doves
Mystic corners hide the pearls
Ancient dolls with yellow curls

Up the creaking stairs
Stacked wooden chairs
Enamel pots on wooden benches
Much to find in the trenches

Medals from fallen heroes
Shine in gilded mirrors
Ivory handles of crafted knives
How many sacrificed lives

Bone buttons in biscuit tins
A gone-bye era of hat pins
Complete the yesteryear picture
With crystal decanters for potent mixture

Luster caricature jugs
Scar the parody of mugs
Petite rose tea sets
Attended by tea-sipping marionettes

Bronze statues pose

Clowns with painted nose
Proud candle sticks of brass
A different time, a different class

Fingers reach out to touch
Eyes drink in much
Soft footsteps creep out
Today no layout

Too much Treasure to comprehend
Leave them together until the end

Musical notes

Musical notes beat against the windowpane
Musical notes beat in my brain
No need for you to explain
Why you sporadically come again
Our need is for you to come again and again

Musical notes beat down on the roof
Musical grey cumulus clouds are proof
Your appearance we all approve

Softly Softly our thirst quench
Softly Softly our ground drench
Softly Softly our livestock caress
Softly Softly you take away our distress
Need for you to impress

Sings our heart with joy
Sings our mind with happiness
Sings our soul – enjoy
We need the healing rain
To wash away our pain

We need food to mouth
For humankind – livestock – north to south
Gone is our hardship – puddles galore

Music to our ears – drip, drip, drip
DEATH – SO FINAL

Death sadly is inevitable. Losing your grandparents, parents, and special friends are tragic. Death leaves you confused and lost. We all have our crosses to bear.

Proud heritage

Lard on my bread
By granny's loving hands spread

Stories of years gone by –
Imagine granny in bonnet and shawl – oh my!

Threading her way through bushes – lamp in hand
Back to the wagon – ready to travel her beloved land

The diamond rush – seemingly chronic
Burying her Ma and Pa in the flu-epidemic

Mischievously transferring the red from the wallpaper
Onto her cheeks in order to look dapper

Wrapping her breasts firmly in bandage –
No fancy brassiere for granny's advantage

Tin of chocolates from General Jan Smuts
"Thank you, South Africa," – his country sure had
guts!

Two twins – one my mother – granny gave birth
Lots of pain – but oh, with so much mirth

Such kind advice – no problem too severe
Such sporting spirit – always there to cheer

Oh Lord – how I miss those deep blue eyes
Endless smiles – oh so wise

Thus Lord, through our love, I now discover
Eternally and afterward we will be part of each
other

What to do now Mom?

Since you've gone, the days have grown
longer, quieter, all of their own
The garden seems to be in shade
Darkening the plants we laid

Seasons come and go
Consumed energy so low
I drive past cemeteries
Inundated with cascading memories
Where are you Mom?

Hurting brain, trying to fathom out death
The finality of your breathe
Our laughter just yesterday so fresh
Now my life filled with so much less

We had our own humor
Eye contact eliminated any intruder
Another birthday has come and gone
Celebrations where you shone
Cheers replaced by tears

Happy time replaced just by years
Eternal optimism disappears
Furrowed brow
Mom – what to do now?

The whistler

I hear your happy whistle in my head
I see you, hands in pocket, taking the lead
I see your smile, the twinkle in your eye
The grey streaks in your hair, your strangely colored
tie

The kindest man I ever knew
Never a bad word against anyone construe
Your love for human beings and animals alike
Your pride deep inside your heart, like a spike

'Give us another song Jo-Jo' – for you no chore
You loved to hear them beg for more
I see you sitting on the arm of the chair
Your beautiful voice filling the room with such flair

Charisma, good looks, warm eyes
Hearing your laughter, my prize
Suddenly your life turned tragic
You lost so much, so drastic

Murder took you away from us – death I was
jealous
Slowly you suffered, we felt helpless
I knew my time with you was running out –
heartache so true

Rest in peace dear father, no one deserves peace
more than you
Your team, my team

You came – I was not ready
Your footsteps I followed – steady
Your eyes awash with the sky
Your team, my team, our trust in my eye

No need to be cautious
Our time so precious
Your friendship so true
My team, your team, our stars askew

Slowly my lessons began
Confidence, laughter, loyalty – courageous man
Difference were a cause for teasing
Your team, my team, our following

Without warning darkness stole my leading light
DIsbelieving tears drench my sight
Thieving drums pound my ears
Your team, my team, no more our cheers

My heart aches with pain
My soul calls your name
Silence and emptiness maimed
Your team, my team, our song forever young again

Lessons over far too soon
Thought I had a lifetime and the moon
Your strength has left me weak
Your team, our team, our friendship peak

I panic – I cannot see your eyes
Now the sky awash with lies
Turn around I plead
Your team, our team, our friendship peak

Forever my senses will seek certainties
Your death, my death
Your team, my team, our memories

My time has come

My time has come
A tune I hum
Dressed in my best garb
Flowing red dress – life's a wrap

Rain has subsided
I've come to the end of my rainbow – already
decided
No friend, No foe, No beau
Just my glow

Clouds descend beyond the light
Dissipating my plight
Guiding me along the path
Leaving life in the aftermath

Green shades of forest
Pruned by 'The Florist'
I catch my last breath
Lay my wreath

I hang up my bag of offerings
Not common things
Valuable worldly possessions
My photograph expressions

I spy white flowers – Purity
Yellow sunrise umbrella - security
The mammoth gates open wide
I stride ahead with pride

Ahead I see the beckoning light
What a sight – so bright
Hasten my footsteps
Clear my mind of subjects

I dance in the puddles with glee
I am free
Oh Lord I come to thee
Such a humble fee

Clock no longer chimes

Time allocated to all humankind
Not tangible – it's all in your mind
Time ticks by slowly but surely
Use your time maturely

Time is not just a clock
Although you can hear the knock
No offer to renew the license
Time is priceless

One commodity you cannot buy
Waste or deplete – too late to cry
Once spent – it's gone forever
Use it wisely – be clever

Plan your life – aims and goals
Ensure they're kind - to sooth our souls
When your time is up
Go gracefully – no occasion to snub

Your clock ticks no longer
Do not grieve – be stronger
Clock no longer chimes
It's time to face your crimes

Death

Death why the stealth?

Arrogant in your claim
With purpose you came
Relentless in your choice
You silenced my voice
Cruel in your timing
My soul is dying
Pain in your thieving
Now I'm grieving

Death – why in my nightmares?

Heartbroken to view the box
Your stalk likened to a fox
Anxious to linger on the last touch
My fingers clutch
Broken to end our memories
There are no remedies
Devastated to close unseeing eyes
My heart cries

Death – why so final?

Troubled at the sudden loss

I bear the cross
Weak at the reality of death
That last breathe
Hurt at all the sorrow
No tomorrow
Confused at the finality
Of your brutality

Death – when do you come for my soul?

When do you take back my spirit?
On what merit?
Who will cry when I am gone?
The children I have spawn?
Where will my spirit go?
With my glow?
Why did I live?
My afterlife – more to give?

OUR LOYAL COMPANIONS

What is a home without a furry animal? We have always had a dog, or two, sometimes three. My youngest son is mainly the culprit. He brings home puppies, proclaiming that the puppy or puppies are his. Then he moves away and leaves the dogs with us.

Gustav was one such dog. When I heard that he had bought a Pit-bull puppy, I was really apprehensive. However he became a fixture in our home. We forgave him for eating our shoes, stealing our socks and pulling washing off the line.

We then bought our own little puppy. A brindle 'Staffie'. We named her Lexi. She was so affectionate and the opposite of Gustav. However they became bosom friends, swimming together, eating together and racing around the outside of the house, taking shortcuts through the house on occasions.

Sadly Gustav, at the age of 13 years old, passed away. Lexi is still with us. She definitely misses old Gustav.

Our furry companions

Irresistible Pit-Bull puppy
Gustav - what a handful and a joy
Cause of missing socks, chewed carpets - bad boy

Black as night, with soulful eyes
White patch on his chest, Superman in disguise
Ferocious bark – no fight

Now grey taints the black
With dismay he limps as Lexi nips his ears
Teasing and tolerance from both throughout the
years

Lexi, brindle Staffie, loving companion
So nimble on her feet, so affectionate
With a super model sway in fashion

A handbag, or a word, alludes to an adventure
A wag and leash in mouth for sure
Ready for car rides or walks of leisure

Both seek out the sun
Gustav sleek, sleeps for fun
While Lexi frolics around him

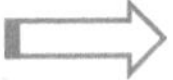

The beach is Lexi's favorite place
Chasing each shell thrown
Rushing the waves on her own

Settling down for the night
Both welcoming their beds so warm
Turning off the lights – our companions who can do
no harm

LIFE IS ALL ABOUT LOVE, LOSS, DEATH, LAUGHTER AND HAPPINESS.

What a mixture! I've had my fair share of each however with regard to love and marriage, I've been very fortunate. I've been married for a long, long, time, to one man. I do admit to trying to kill him on occasion but thankfully I was unsuccessful.

Love and marriage

We were married so young
Nonetheless you became my hero unsung
Together we built a life, a home
Then to our delight we became a foursome

Fretting I trudged my way through motherhood
You always there to ensure they reached adulthood
Soccer coach, rugby, rowing, you on the sideline
Cheering our boys on, ensuring they were fine

Supporting me throughout my career
Albeit with a little coercion from me dear
Nothing I asked was too much for you
My life without you – I have no clue

Passionate altercations we certainly had
I remember being so mad
I planned your murder in my head
You having to duck otherwise dead

Now we celebrate another anniversary
45 and counting – grandchildren in the nursery
You are my best friend, and protector
You the financial director, me the managing
director

Having a sense of humor, to one another being kind
is definitely the type of marriage we designed
Not perfect, never easy, but we made it work
Now I can afford to sit back and smirk

The heart of the moon

Heart weeps at loss of knight
Curse the moonlight
Love blossomed on your watch Luna
Now his heart hardened lava

Far from Planet Earth
You watch with mirth
Play cupid celestial body
Heartbreaker you embody

Outshine all the satellites
Darkness hide the moonlight nights
Traitorous tides cause reflection
Crushing young affection

White, Yellow, Greys of every hue
Transform your magic coat on cue
Thief, you played your part
Give me back my heart

Our hearts were captured in part
Gravity force – master-of-art
My heart you kept – his heart you released
Last rites for me Priest

Blood red roses

I sent you long stemmed red roses
As a symbol of my affection
As a symbol of love's reflection
I wanted nothing but your love in return
What I received instead was your scorn

I decorated your garden with fairy lights
Your driveway I scattered with red rose petals
Your sarcastic answer was clear in your letters
You smirked – turning your back
Empathy, my dear, you lack

I removed the thorns – my blood red
Not enough – you wanted more – for you I bled
You made it clear - Diamonds and Pearls
Glitter and glamour is what your heart yearns
My pockets are empty

Now I see you with someone new
How fickle – if only I knew
Laden with jewelry
You obliterate my optimistic memory
Now I pity your 'someone new'

Angel love

You called me angel
Title of Fallen Angel I dangle
Destroyer of Love

You held me in your arms
I broke free of your charms

You loved me with all your heart
I ripped your heart apart

Your brain told you to give me time
Not in this lifetime

Your hands reached out to me
I had to flee

Disdainful am I
Avenging Angel of my own lie
Destroyer of Love

Deceitful abuse

Invitation to the warmth of your home
Cloaked in secret deceit
My faith you delete

The warmth of your heart
Pure manipulation
I should have proceeded with caution

You drenched me in your smell
Too late I sensed the smell of misconstruction
Or was it my misconception?

Enveloped in the false friendship of your arms
I rested my head against your cunning body
The devil in you embody

Did I aid your pretense?
My fists beat your heart
You thought you were smart

Now I scream in this cold room
No warmth here to sooth my ache
Soon my wake

Murder has no warmth
Treacherous cold body
Your cruel jokes, my malady

Lead me away with chains
to my resting place
where my revenge will find grace

The beggar

The gaunt face stares with hope as the busy people
pass him by
No time to stop, everyone in a hurry, no time to cry
Everyone is going somewhere, he is going nowhere
He was one of these busy people, with a career and
loved ones so fair
Now he sits alone, humiliated, sad and needy

The thin body shivers against the cold wind
Huddling closer to the concrete support so unkind
Passersby snuggle deeper into their fashionable
coats
Feet encased in warm boots, in their belly warm
oats
Avoiding the weather, avoiding the man with the
sad eyes

Then someone takes the time to stop
Someone hands him a hot cup of soup from the
busy food shop
The beggar gives the man a charming smile
Intelligence radiates from his eyes as he thanks the
stranger in kind profile
The stranger rushes off to avoid the intelligence in
the beggar's eyes

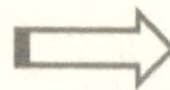

The stranger feels sad and confused
How does an intelligent, charming man become
homeless, so bruised?
This thought scares the stranger, he shivers with
unease
He thinks of his wife, children, his career, material
belongings, earned with ease
How could that all be taken away from one?

The gaunt eyes recognizes the stranger's confusion
He knows the questions in his head – life's an
illusion
Reality dictates, his seat can be taken by anyone
Hurt and fate are a powerful combination when life
is done
When dreams turn to nightmares

The mental struggle becomes too much
Apathy replaces faith, turns your back on touch
Emptiness fills your soul
Loss of confidence tears your heart and leaves a
hole
Homeless – a condition of circumstance – not
choice

HAPPINESS – LAUGHTER IS THE MEDICINE

As I said before life is also about happiness, learning to laugh at yourself and at life itself. Music was a happy constant throughout my life, and still is.

The chauffeur

Stylish woman you summon me
I arrive for passengers three
Children jump with glee
Mrs Jones ready for a shopping spree

My aging undergoes the best therapy
I feel young, carefree and happy
Many distances I have drove
Today I found my treasure trove

Their laughter cuts through my depression
Their eyes full of compassion
They know Mrs Jones treats me badly
However I drive on boldly

Our journey comes to an end
To Mrs Jones I extend my hand
Shrieking she falls to the gutter
I hear her curse and mutter

I guess the swipe and the sway
Resulted in a messy day
For Mrs Jones

Music – my constant companion

Music fills my soul
Revokes sad nostalgia, invokes happy memories
Lyrics resonate unspoken words, unspoken stories
Long forgotten emotions – why?
Friends from days gone by
Creep into my mind, creep into my eye

Play me a song to change my mood
Speak to my heart lyrics – don't be cruel
Strum my emotions - the harmony of senses rule
Whistle to life's melody
Tap to the beat physically and mentally
Creep into my psyche, creep into my destiny

Forlorn, joyful, expression of art
Bring me back to my happy place
Communicate peace to grant me grace
Contentment of soul to sing along
Out of tune – voice true and strong
Creep into my spirit, creep into my theme song

Music legends – I give my thanks
Elvis, Rod Stewart – you rock
Barbra Streisand, Amy Winehouse – the way they
were
Ediaf Piaf – emotion defer
Every word understood
Music – my constant companion since childhood

YOGA DAYS

When we moved to Mossel Bay in the Cape Province
I realized that I was terribly unfit from all the sitting
at a corporate desk.

That and no exercise. I decided to start a new diet –
again – and join a gym. Aerobics was definitely not
an option. Too much jumping around. I gleefully
joined Yoga, thinking that the exercises seemed easy
enough. Well I was mistaken. However a year later I
am slightly thinner and definitely fitter.

Amateur yogi am I

I arrive for my weekly yoga class
Lurking about I fear I trespass
At the door appears my ultimate goal
Armed with a breakfast bowl
Blond, gorgeous, supple, and dammit, kind
To my body type and mind I am resigned
To master so many attributes
Cruel states of consciousness disputes

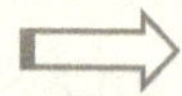

Second goal is physical fitness
I'm superwoman – fearless
The books promise a remedy for anti-aging
My bones creek, muscles aching
Now I need to reduce my stress
First the wooden block I must caress
It's all-out war against the zombie apocalypse
I squeeze my buttocks and gingerly lift my hips

I'm fully prepared to tackle Asana
Perhaps I can ask for her banana
Next stance my legs and arms resist
Hurriedly I go through my checklist
My core needs strengthening
Unfortunately I'm busy wrestling
with my toes on the mat
Thank goodness for my strap

I try the mountain poses
The wall no bed of roses
Standing position, Plank or Tree
Thank goodness no camera for me
Mastering backbends I long
for that damn bird to stop his song
for control of Pranayama
without all my melodrama

More Meditation and less monkey brain ⇨

I will not complain
Next week I'll be back again

Food for thought

On my back I look to the heavens
Conjuring up inspired impressions
Pale blue palette stares back at me
Body and soul experience the feeling of being free
Sky smudged by white scattered clouds
No chaos, no noise, no crowds

Imaginative images start forming in my mind
There's my dog skipping toward a small boy, so kind
The kneeling boy holds out his tiny hand
They are way up there while I'm on land
An elderly lady points her walking stick
Toward the pair, apologies, it's a broomstick

Such tranquility, calm filters through my body
Thankfully, I need this antibody
Creative juices flow in my veins
None of my pitiless thought remains
The Artists' palette a feast
All my anxiety released

Overhead I hear a light aircraft
In the sky he signs his autograph
Startled I hear the Hadida as they call out
To their feathered friends on route
Their call so loud and distinctive
This freedom I will not relinquish

I want to be thin

I want to be thin
I'm just a few kilo's overweight, complete with
double chin
My doctor disagrees with the word 'few'

I try to follow a balanced diet
Then we join friends for an outing – what a riot
Everyone is eating burgers with fresh fries

I try not to drink wine
Everyone's glasses are filled with the spoils of the
vine
I feel silly with my glass of water

To add to my dilemma
My scale is a relic from another era
Temperamental – a different reading from day to
day

I resort to checking my shadow
I try different angles – what a low blow
Not one angle reflects a tall, thin model

My other problem is my height
If I were eight inches taller, what a sight
My plight to be skinnier would be so much easier

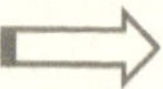

I decide to join Yoga
Eighty year old, shame my stances – I'm in a coma
I should have taken up belly dancing

As a last resort I listen avidly to audio tapes
Persuading voluptuous women to accept their
shapes
I think I'm actually starting to lose weight!

Malevolent age

Youth poses arrogantly
Youth waits patiently
Youth gives age no credence
Youth screams in abundance

Hope comes to closure
Hope realizes time gone for sure
Hope has time to cry
Hope cringes at time to die

Guilt you pound at youth fading
Guilt you scorn the onset of aging
Guilt you turn your back on aging process
Guilt you refuse the aging game of chess

Pain looks age in the mirror
Pain recognizes the slur
Pain turns away
Pain confronts age every day

Age – now arrogant, takes place impatiently
Age- the mirror awaits scornfully

AS A CLOSING NOTE, BE HAPPY – ENJOY LIFE!

The secret to life

To be content is our mission
To have peace in your mind paramount
We all have dreams and ambition
The need to fulfil our passions tantamount

The truth will set you free
Lies eat away at your conscious
Spread your roots – stand tall and firm as a tree
With your tongue be cautious

Follow your survival instincts with verve
Tackle tasks with a steady nerve
Have fun and light your own fires
I wish for you whatever your hear desires

SHORT STORIES BY SHARON BRUMMER

In the afterlife

An optimistic pinkish dusk slowly morphed into a dark, windy night. Lieutenant Charles Alexander, clad in his bright red British army jacket, marched out of 66 Lager House, trying to escape to scorn of his roommate, Smitty. Passing Searles Manor made him feel uncomfortable. Men like Searle and Joseph Vincent represented the hierarchy of the ultra-rich and powerful. Searles Manor was in the process of being built. Stone masons had stacked large square quarry stones, ready for the erection of an architectural gem.

Charles' head bowed before the swirling wind. He cursed the slither of a moon which cast little light on the dusty streets. Dotted around the warehouse to his left were large cast iron street oil lamps which painted grotesque shadows looming over him. As he approached the cemetery, he purposely looked in the opposite direction, turning sharply past the jail. Staggering along Marsh Street he tried not to peak into the windows of Mr Mudie's stately home. In that home was the woman he loved. May returned that love. Mr Mudie however was determined to keep them apart. To date he had not been successful.

At last he reached the foot of the intimidating hill, leading to the St Blaize caves, and then onto the St Blaize Lighthouse. He stopped to drink lustily from his hip flask. He had shopped earlier at the 'Stones' liquor store. There he had purchased rather a large quantity of the infamous "Sakkies". He loved the taste of the sweet red wine.

Zigzagging up the hill, Charles finally reached his goal. Sitting on a large rock he looked out to treacherous sea. He watched as the waves crashed, into the rocks, at the foot of the harbor. With every crash, his heart ached. Looking around he prayed for May to arrive. The black night engulfed Charles. He was surrounded by squawking birds, teasing him as he waited with tainted breath. Charles felt anxiety tear at his senses. His heart and soul were empty without her. Every day he waited impatiently for nightfall. Damn Mr Mudie. Damn the powerful Free Masons. They had warned him to leave May alone and not to continue his courtship of her. They taunted him, calling him a drunk and a man devoted to seduction.

The air suddenly became cold and eerie, and then she was there, smiling and turning the dark night into a shimmering silver oasis. Long black hair twirled around her. Charles was happy just to embrace her, without any words. His dark mood transformed into a habitually smiling face. He would lend an attentive ear. He would flatter May with words of devotion. She looked so innocent and childlike in her white linen, flowing dress. Earlier he had dismissed Smitty playfully calling him a conceited handsome man. In his opinion he was a genteel man of noble descent. A man in love with the most beautiful, captivating, woman on earth. He would fight to the death for her. She belonged to him.

The 'hoi polloi' be damned. He was no maudlin drunk. They could continue to ridicule him with mock salutes and call him 'Leftenant'. Bollocks to them. They probably partook in opium, whilst listening to Beethoven's 5th symphony.

Charles spent loving hours with May, sheltered by the caves. The air around them electric. Ugly thoughts of her father creeping into his psyche. That man had tormented his soul, wanting May to spurn his affection.

Long after May had left, Charles still savored her glow. He stared at the perilous rock-face around him, shaking off a nagging spine-chilling realization. An ominous foreboding. His heart would not listen to his brain. Shrugging his broad shoulders, he made his way down the hazardous hill, toward the hostel. By now his hip flask was empty.

Earlier that night Smitty had begged Charles to stay and dine with him. The conversation had not gone well.

"Though ever so willing, I cannot Smitty." Charles had advised his friend. "I have a previous engagement which I can no longer stall."

"Do you say the real truth in speaking to me? Shouted Smitty. "I think not, kind Sir. I shall be obliged if you stay with me, this dark and dreary night."

"I give you my word, dear friend. I too am knackered, however this engagement I have to keep."

"Give me your attention Sir. Stay and explain to me where, and who, you have an engagement with."

"I cannot linger Smitty. I take leave of you good friend. Do not fret. I shall be back before your dreams take place."

Flashing his charismatic smile, Charles had taken leave of Smitty.

With labored breath, Charles approached 66 Lager houses. A surreal light seemed to illuminate the hostel. He could hear horses snorting from the stables of the warehouse. The stench was overwhelming. He dismissed the stench. On his jacket he could smell May's scent. A fragrance of love.

If he had been more astute, he would have detected a bulky shadow following him. Charles dragged his tired body up the stairs to his room. Opening the door, he noted Smitty fast asleep. Without warning he felt a huge hand clamp over his mouth. The strength of the arm around him, held him in a metal grip. Then he felt a sharp object penetrate his kidneys, and then his chest. Charles slumped to the floor with a thud. No sound emanating from his limp body.

Smitty woke up, startled. Struggling out of bed, he saw the lifeless body of Charles lying in a pool of blood, on the wooden floor. Dark red blood stained Charles' blond gleaming hair, darkening his jaunty red coat. Blue eyes stared blankly at Smitty. Instantly he knew his earlier premonition had materialized.

Mr Mudie hurried down the stairs of 66 Lager house, into the dark streets of Mossel Bay. He avoided all lit areas until he reached his home. There he viewed the gaunt silhouette of his wife in the sash windows. He leaned heavy against the corrugated railing. Taking a deep breath, he entered the house where his wife helped him burn his clothes in the roaring fireplace. After washing and dressing, Mr Mudie strode toward the Masonic temple. There he would be safe. There were no windows. There his powerful 'Free Mason' friends awaited him. They would represent a tight clad alibi on this dark revengeful night.

A secret handshake welcomed him into the temple. Powerful men approached him. One of them handed Mr Mudie a whisky, which he gulped down. They had all agreed that taking revenge on Charles Alexander was paramount. Mr Mudie had buried his only daughter, May, just two weeks ago. She had committed suicide after their house doctor had confirmed that at 19 years old, she was five months pregnant. She had wanted to marry Charles Alexander and keep the baby. What would Mossel Bay upper class have to say? Panicked, debating their next move, they tried to keep her prisoner. A maid's traitorous note had May escaping to meet Charles. However Charles had lingered too long at 'Stones'. Bereft and fretful May climbed up the rugged ridge above the St Blaize caves, just below the lighthouse, jumping to her death.

All the Mudie's had now, was a gravesite to visit. Devastated they had buried May in her white flowing linen dress. Her favorite.

Charles Alexander was given a full military funeral, with a three gun salute. The funeral service was carried out at the majestic stone Anglian Church, built by the stone masons from Cornwall. The steeple, made of solid stone, reached high into the dark cumulous clouds, seemingly to mock them. The pallbearers had all worn gloves. They did not want Charles Alexander's spirit entering their body. Trouble always seemed to follow him, and now look where he lay.

His body was taken by a horse-drawn hearse, to the cemetery. Charles Alexander was buried in the English section of the graveyard, ten steps from May Mudie's grave. Smitty was devastated. He had known that the Free Mason's would take revenge against Charles. The travelling magistrate however had deemed the murder a mystery. Mr Mudie was not a suspect. He had concrete alibis, upheld by the most prominent men in Mossel Bay.

Ironically, on May's headstone the inscription read 'United we shall be in death.' Mr Mudie did not realize that the inscription now applied to May and

Charles. Their spirits were united. At last they could be together without interference from anyone. Charles smelt May's scent. He knew she was within a few feet of him. Now who was able to throw scorn in the face of Mr Mudie.

On dark ghostly nights, the residents near the cemetery complain about a young couple traipsing around the cemetery, laughing. She in her white linen dress, he in full British military regalia. Other nights it is quiet, as lovers tend to behave.

If only the baby would stop crying.

The hairdresser

Armed with scissors, comb and a strong cup of coffee, I start my new day. Every day poses a new challenge with the onslaught of new clientele who visit the salon. My feet, firmly squeezed into a fashionable pair of flats, confirm I'm ready for the long hours of hair dressing and psychology consultations. I often suggest to the owner that we should have couches in the salon. We can then charge extra for the psychology sessions.

People from all walks of life enter our doors. Excitement fills the air when 'The Kardashians' of Mossel Bay enter the salon. The three siblings declare loudly that they want to look like Kylie Jenner. They are not triplets. Sparkling claws adorn their chubby fingers which they use to emphasize the importance of looking like Kylie. They have various magazine covers portraying Kylie Jenner just in case we are not aware of who she is.

Their extra-long extended eyelashes flutter up and down, in sync with the exclamation marks made by their claws. They pout, they strut their well-endowed butts in the mirror, and prop up their silicone cleavage. Red puffy lips point out mother dear, who has arrived huffing and puffing. Obviously, she finds it difficult to keep up with these girls.

Perhaps the reason why she parked in the disabled parking bay.

Mom's lips are so puffy, it's difficult to decipher what she is saying. She wants to look like Kaitlyn Jenner. Panic sets in, my scissor is frozen in mid-air. I sigh with relieve when she explains that she is often mistaken for Kris Jenner and therefore must have the same cut and color.

I smile and agree with her. My face hurts from all the fake smiling. Her face is as small as a teacup. Her hair is thinning and stringy. Hopefully I can achieve a miracle today with my magic wand. I order another cup of coffee, silently wishing for a tequila.

Their pitch black 'microblade-eyebrows' will certainly aid me in my plight to reincarnate 'The Kardashian' look, as well as the extended eyelashes which seem to hold up their foreheads. The three sisters talk in high pitch voices, checking the mirrors, to ensure that everyone in the salon is listening to them. Their dialogues are a constant stream of verbal diarrhea. They complain about the sound of the hair dryers. The owner reminds them they are in a hair salon. They dismiss her explanation by shrugging their shoulders and raising their voices above the hair dryers. Our other clients look confused, amused, and gob smacked, all at the same time. The owner rushes around to supply coffee to all the clients, assuring them that their time in the salon will soon come to an end. She also hands out cotton wool for their ears.

Deep breaths and we plunge into the verminous process. Mom plumbs up her silicone breasts and starts divulging all her secrets of success. She stresses that she has an image to uphold as her husband is a prominent member of Mossel Bay. She reminds all that she is an expert at entertaining and her tan is absolutely authentic, courtesy of their yacht. Not only do they have a yacht, but the kids have their own jet skis. She insists I look through the photos on her phone. There are hundreds. There are so many, I constantly have to wet my finger with spit, just to be able to keep sliding the numerous photos on and on. How do you take a Selfie whilst driving a jet ski?

She also reminds me that the rich and famous will be seeing their hair styles, at their scheduled party this evening. If the hair styles do not meet their standards, there could be adverse repercussions for the salon, and for myself. I silently pray that they find another victim.

Next to me I can hear my colleagues' heavy breathing. The girls are being pedantic, rude and opinionated. Mom pretends she cannot hear them. I feel badly for my colleague's and give them a sympathetic smile. They roll their eyes. They've been here before. There is no cure. You have to live through the hurricane until the storm moves on to another area. The owner phones the nearby restaurant to warn them of the ambush they are about to experience. She peers out, noticing a 'Closed' sign being hung on the door. Their reputation precedes them. I can hear security doors being double locked all around the small shopping center. Everyone has gone on an early lunch.

In the mirror, their facial expressions, are already complaining about the length of the process. I start dreaming of tomorrow. Aunt Susie is coming for her weekly appointment. She always tells me wonderful, amusing stories of her grandchildren. Her reminiscing always takes me back to my childhood and happy memories.

All three girls are now pouting for Selfies, fingers flying across their iPhones as they post their ordeal on Instagram. Strutting around the salon, they use the many mirrors to check the results. Even mother dear has her skinny buttocks in the mirror, hands on hips, as she strides towards the till. The smile disappears when presented with the full bill. She complains loudly for some time, gesturing at her purse and encouraging the other salon clients to back her up. To no avail. Finally she pays the bill and stalks out of the salon, followed by the rest of her chicks.

We all sigh with relief, even our clients. We then hear them trying to break into the various security doors of the adjoining shops and restaurants. The mall has become a ghost town. Eventually they make their way back to the disabled parking spot. All four women glare at the security guard in case he questions their reasoning for parking in the disabled parking bay. He pretends he has just received a phone call on his cell, his head nodding nervously. His eyes averted just in case they are planning to argue with him. Stealthy he skulks away, ashamed at his cowardice.

I stumble up the stairs to my apartment. What a day. What a challenge. Only once inside do I finally feel safe from the mafia family. I put the kettle on while I throw back a quick tequila. I remind myself that tequila has many medicinal benefits. I kick my shoes off and slump onto a chair. Off comes the wig ...Thank goodness... It is so hot and uncomfortable. The tufts of thinning hair on my head stick up in all directions. Talk about perfect hair styles.

Undressing I look in the mirror. Laughing I realize I resemble a caricature of my previous self. Soon I too will have to consider reconstructive surgery on my breasts. I may have to ask 'The Kardashians' who their plastic surgeon is. Cancer has taken both my breasts. A real life challenge, not unlike a hurricane which swirls around and then comes back when you least expect it. Dealing with 'The Kardashians' is just a temporary challenge to my skills with the scissors. Fortunately tomorrow will be another day and hopefully I will live to tell another hairdresser story.

Breaking free of the shackles

Emma examined her face in the mirror. Day old bruises had turned purple and green. She could definitely not go shopping in this condition. Not even sunglasses would hide her swollen face.

She looked further than the bruises, examining the spirit looking back at her. Where was the once vibrant, confident, woman? Blank, accusing, eyes stared back at her. Her soul had retreated. Mourning her lost spirit and soul, Emma went in search of her wedding photo album. She traced the smiling faces with her fingers. They had only known each other for such a short time. Emma had never believed in love at first sight, but meeting Brad, changed all that. He had swept her off her feet with his ease of charm, good looks, and intelligence. At first, he had been kind, attentive and tolerant. Emma now knew that he was a narcissist. His gifts had been bribes. His kindness a cloak for his possessiveness. He wanted to possess. He wanted control of all his assets, including Emma.

In her naivetés, Emma initially saw a life of everlasting adventures and travel. Brad had described the world as his oyster. However that oyster had become her prison.

Each time they ventured out; Emma's life was turned upside down. If she turned her head in the direction of a male, she had surely committed adultery. No matter the poor man's age or disposition. An argument would secure some form of emotional abuse, which would last for days.

As the months progressed, so did the physical abuse. Resigning from her successful career sadly did not relief Emma from being accused of betrayal. Friends of long-standing stopped visiting. They could see the trauma and fear in Emma's eyes. They could read Brad's attempt at total control of Emma. He did not want friends around. He wanted to possess her in every way possible.

Emma loaded the wash machine. For a 26 year old her movements were painfully labored. The rest of the house had been cleaned meticulously. Brad would expect a spotless house, an empty wash basket, and a well-balanced meal, on the table, when he returned from work. Anything less would result in an altercation, and an elaborate explanation of Emma's itinerary for that particular day. He wanted her to account for every minute of the day. Each of those minutes had to be spent on Brad's needs. Never her needs.

Tired and depressed, Emma closed the wedding album. That day had marked the end of her happiness. The very next day she had been confronted with the truth. Instead of spending a few days with her parents, as originally planned, Brad had decided that they should go home immediately. Shock and realization had slowly but surely set in. He had been adamant and brutal about their immediate departure. Brad's true colors had not taken long to make their harsh appearance. Emma had not seen her parents since that miserable day. She acknowledged that no longer was she that youthful, exuberant woman.

A degree in psychology had not been able to rescue her. Facing the mirror once more, she saw a coward. Emma felt ashamed. She hid her in a face in her hands.

Reaching for her cellphone, Emma suddenly remembered that Brad had been monitoring her calls. Any phone calls, or unexplained delays when shopping, would result in a full out onslaught. Sinking to the floor, Emma finally allowed her tears to flow freely. She sobbed, thus admitting defeat. She could no longer be this woman. She was better than this. She was stronger. Time was on her side. She had the time to turn her life around. She would start again. Far, far, away from Brad. Thoughts about being able to change him were no longer viable.

In the bedroom she pulled out two large suitcases. Packing her bare essentials took Emma two precious hours. She left behind the jewelry Brad had bought her, including her wedding rings. She also left behind all the clothing he had spoilt her with whilst dating, including her wedding dress. On her bed lay their dreaded wedding album. She did not need anything to remind her of Brad. A wasted year of her life. She wanted to break free of his shackles.

Loading her car, Emma heaved a sigh of relief. Soon she would be free. The car had been the one and only item, Brad had allowed her to keep. Now it would serve as her means of escape.

Before she could climb into the vehicle, her cellphone rang. It was Brad. Calmly she answered his questions, silently making a note to destroy the phone before leaving. As usual he apologized profusely for the argument the previous evening, laboring on about how much he loved her. Emma was surprised at her unwavering voice and her acting skills. She told him she loved him, and that they would have a romantic dinner when he arrived home. Blowing kisses into the phone, she finally settled herself into the seat of the vehicle. As she drove away, she did not look back.

After driving for an hour, Emma heard a patrol vehicle's sirens. Emma slowed down, pulling to the side of the road. Anxiety gripped her tightly. Alighting from the car, the officer examined Emma's swollen and bruised face. He apologized, explaining that her husband had reported her missing, as well as the car. An alarm went off in Emma's head. Brad must have planted a tracker in her vehicle. Emma assured the officer that she was definitely not missing. In fact, for the first time in a year, she had finally found herself, and shed her shackles. She knew he understood what she was saying.

Stepping back the officer again apologized. He encouraged her to carry on with her journey, and to drive safe. He had also asked whether she wanted to lay charges of assault against anyone. Both of them knew who the 'anyone' was. Emma smiled but shook her head. All she wanted was to obliterate her year of marriage. Lesson learnt.

Suddenly a car screeched to a halt, blocking her path. Startled she stared at the one person she thought she had left behind. Brad. His face was black with anger. He jumped out of his vehicle, spitting and frothing at the mouth. The officer put his hand forward to stop Brad from advancing toward Emma. Brad changed his direction of attack, turning instead toward the officer. The officer reached for his gun. Emma suddenly noticed that Brad was armed. An automatic handgun was pointed direct at the officer. Still shouting abuse at Emma, Brad pulled the trigger, before the officer could reach his own gun. The officer fell backwards, blood already painting the tarred road. Another young life wasted. Gone forever, not just for a year, and it was her fault.

Then Brad turned his gun toward Emma. Blocking out Brad's ranting, she faced him with no fear in her eyes. She could see his surprise. At the same time she realized her flight was over. Her mistake in marrying him would result in her losing more than just one year. Finally Emma's torturous journey was over. She had left too late. She felt remorse for her parents, for the life she was originally destined to live. Emma would never realize her full potential.

Brad's handsome face turned crimson as he fired the gun again. She wanted to see something other than his face as the life drained out of her. She would not give him the last victory. Turning her head, she smiled at the young officer. His blank eyes stared back at Emma. Then Emma's world went dark as sirens swirled around them.

Emma did not die on this day. She died on the day of her wedding. Brad had lost the one possession he could not control. He felt betrayed. Facing the news' cameras, he saw his image reflected back at him. Handcuffed he smiled. He saw a good looking, charming young man, who had been wronged. He had not killed Emma. The jury would believe him. He knew he would soon be a free man. In the meantime he would enjoy the fame and attention.

With your hand in mine

Rosa scrutinized her image in the gilded mirror. The large, full length mirror revealed a tall, slim, woman, in Flamengo stance. Her posture so strong and erect, her brown eyes full of passion and fascination. Her arms curved perfectly above her head. Raven black hair cascaded down her arched back. She looked stunning and she knew it.

Rosa then examined her dress. The blood red garment clung to her curves, ending in voluminous frills which teased her black shoes decorated with red flowers. Rosa was glowing. Tonight's performance would be electrifying. For her, Juan, and the audience. As usual the audience would honor the Spanish dance sequence by throwing roses onto the stage. The stage-hand would collect all the flowers, placing them in vases, all over Rosa's dressing room. The scent was intoxicating and well deserved for both of them.

Looking once more at her reflection in the mirror, she turned her head. Over her right shoulder she saw Juan. He offered her a slow, seductive smile. His body just as arched. He sat on a wooden stool, armed with a Spanish guitar. Curly black hair made him look younger than his 26 years. Mischievous green eyes danced with celebration. Song, dance, and music. Both of them marked each occasion with a celebration. This is what they lived for. Their passion for each other, the opportunity to dance, and make music, for the ultimate Flamengo. A celebration of love.

Juan took Rosa's hand in his, kissing her fingertips, before he took hold of his guitar. He strummed his guitar, shaping the cords with his expertise. Rosa clapped her hands to the beat. Then her feet started a rhythmic stamping all of their own volition. The rhythm was part of her soul. Her spirit felt each step without her mind's command. The beat guided her feet and her arms, strumming the air with each note. She was lost in the potent atmosphere.

The words of the song, sang by Juan, were verses of love and loss, punctuated by guitar interludes. A lust for love. His guitar took on a sense of urgency, spilling out emotions of life. Rosa's body twisted as her own emotions intensified. Her facial expressions reflecting the intensity of Juan's music. His voice haunting, as she watched him in the mirror.

A thin bead of perspiration broke out on Juan's forehead. He looked so vulnerable, yet so strong and in command. He was now totally devoted to his art. Rosa knew he sensed her but could not see her. Her rhythmic pattern slowed down as she sensually rolled her hips. For the first time she smiled, also slowly and seductively. By now she would have the audience eating out of her hands.

Rosa shrugged the shawl off her shoulders. The flowered fringed shawl fell to the ground. Lightning-fast footwork matched the tapping of Juan's black boots against the stool. His black-string pants drenched with sweat. This was the best tonic for love. Juan gave the guitar his full attention. His fingers flying over the tight strings, picking away at the tune. Rosa kept up the tempo. Her feet mimicking his palm against the body of the guitar. Her body felt every touch and caress. Together they cast a magic spell. A magic spell in which both of them, and their audience, were lost in desire for more. More dance. More music. More song.

Suddenly Rosa's mind was thrown back in time. A magical time of youth. Love between Rosa and Juan had blossomed when they were still teenagers. Both had lived in the same, quaint village in Southern Spain. Both grey up amidst folklore music traditions where Flamengo dances were the norm. Wherever they went, Juan always carried his battered guitar. When all the string were finally broken, he beat the rhythm against the battered wood. Rose smiled, thinking of their yesteryear love. She had been so innocent and naïve, not realizing that Juan had already decided that Rosa's hand, in marriage, would be his.

They had fought as teenagers, they had fought as grown-ups, with as much passion as they had made love. They were one.

Juan and Rosa were married to the delight of their aging parents. The married couple moved closer to the city where they could work and study. Juan studied music, happily purchasing his first brand new Spanish guitar. The Sycamore wood of the guitar shone with pride. Again Juan carried his guitar wherever they went. No occasion was too insignificant for him to bring out his guitar. Flirtatiously he would extend his hand to his beautiful Rosa, and then together they would weave their magic, until well after their audience had dispersed.

Rosa heard a noise behind her. Turning she saw her instructor. Thick grey hair, paired with intelligent green eyes, gave him a dignified air. His body, though aged, was still strong and proud. He approached her with an upright posture, measuring his footsteps. Rosa was not sure of his age, but he still struck an impressive figure in the studio. Now he smiled at her gently, encouraging her to continue with her dance. Suddenly she felt tired. Looking around she noticed Juan had left the room. He had taken her energy with him. She mourned the loss. Confused she noticed her matronly aide entering the room.

Judging the aide immediately, Rosa became irritated with the woman. Her temper flared. She felt as though she could smack the woman. This woman had no grace, no pride, and no rhythm. She was certainly an undignified creature to behold. Slouching she walked with her head lolling to one side.

"Oh for goodness sake woman, square your shoulders! Walk with your head held high! Pick up your feet! Do not dare shuffle in front of me!" Rosa's voice was loud and aggressive.
"Sorry Rosa", repented the middle aged woman. She looked at Rosa with love and concern in her eyes. Her lips thin in distress.

"Put a smile on that face woman. You look as though you are carrying the weight of the world on your shoulders."
The woman conceded, smiling pleasantly at Rosa.

"That's better. No slouching in my studio. Especially when Juan and I are practicing for an important stage performance. Which is tonight my dear. Time is of the essence."
"Your shawl Rosa." Offered the woman.

She handed Rosa the shawl. Looking down Rosa noticed that the shawl was tatty and faded. The once vibrant frills were now sad looking. The rose pattern hardly visible.

"Oh dear", said Rosa in a voice ringing with confusion rather than confidence, "I think I need a new shawl. I cannot go on stage tonight with this shawl. What's your name dear lady? You will have to shop for a new shawl immediately."

"Rosa, my name is Isabella. The shops are closed today. We'll have to buy you a new shawl tomorrow."

"That will be too late for our performance."
Rosa's voice rose in panic. Isabella and the instructor rushed over to pacify her. Confused and panic stricken, Rosa looked around the room. Two plain single beds stood against a white bare wall. Two armchairs, and a small table took up the rest of the stark room. In the corner stood a battered guitar.
She stretched out her strong arms to the grey haired man. He held her gently against his frail chest, smoothing her long grey hair with his bony fingers. Years of strumming his beloved guitar, coupled with the onset of ruthless aging, had disfigured his hands. Arthritis had claimed his once agile fingers.

Rosa laid her head on his chest. This felt familiar to her. The room and Isabella, foreign. Her mind told her that if she closed her eyes for long enough, the gilded mirror would once again bring the studio and a youthful Juan back to her. She ached for the music. Her soul felt empty. Her spirit had fled.

Opening her eyes, Rosa looked outside of the window. It must be autumn she thought. An array of colored leaves were falling to the ground, only to the scooped up into the air by the swirling wind.

"It's too cold to go outside Mom. Sit and I'll read to you and Dad."

This was a strange world thought Rosa. Why was she in this sparsely decorated room? Was the distinguished, grey haired man really Juan? His touch and smile certainly felt familiar. Did she really have a daughter... With such bad posture? Trying to regain some dignity and clarity, Rosa examined her attire. Grey! A grey pleated dress with matching grey shoes. She obviously had not shopped for such dreary clothes. What happened to her beautiful black shoes with red roses? She fingered her pleated dress. Her world had suddenly turned grey.

"What's wrong with me?" Rosa asked with intelligent eyes on both Juan and Isabella.

Juan stepped forward, taking her hands in his.

"We are old Rosa. We have grown old together. We still love each other. I could never live without you Rosa. I'll never leave you. We'll be together forever." Juan passionately reassured Rosa.

"Mom, you are suffering from dementia. You forget things. You always forget you have a daughter... Me." said Isabella in an accusing but gentle voice. "Sometimes you still think you're a Flamengo dancer. Those memories must be extremely strong."

Isabella thought to herself that those memories were the one thing keeping both her mother and father alive. Rosa could be a handful. At times she was depressed, at times aggressive and demanding.

Rosa appealed to Juan, wanting his reassurance, "Juan, I saw you. You were sitting on your favorite stool, strumming your guitar. I was dancing to your beat Juan, as I usually do. Juan I was wearing my favorite red dress."

"I know Rosa. Those memories will always be with us. Not even dementia can take those memories away from you. I watch you reenacting your dance sequence. I envisage what you see. I share those memories with you. The entire sequence. Memories come so freely to you. You get to relive a wonderful time in our lives. We are lucky. Otherwise our hours would be so long, so empty."

"Am I a bother to you Juan?"

"Never my love. Your enactment of our memories transport you back in time. Such an exciting time in our lives. They keep you young and beautiful Rosa."

"What happened to our studio……To our performances?"
"That's all gone Rosa. We live a simple life now in an old age home where nursing staff care for you… For us. Growing old is difficult Rosa. Fortunately we have Isabella. She is a good and caring daughter."

"I'm sorry Isabella. I don't remember you." Rosa's voice held a weight of sadness. Gone was the arrogant, confident woman.
Isabella stared at her mother. She was having a moment of clarity. She was piecing things together in her head. Isabella could see the awakening in her mother's eyes. Her father was right, Rosa was still a beautiful woman.

"It's alright Mom. There are days that you do remember me. Those are special days but every day I spend with you is precious. Do not fret." Isabella spoke softly to her mother. She could see her distress and sadness. Rosa's transformation occurred often. From a passionate young Flamengo dancer, to an aged woman with dementia. Her father had such patience.

How he coped with Rosa on a daily basis was a miracle. He truly loved her. Some days she lay immobilized in her bed. Her mind totally blank. Her father would then sing to Rosa to soothe her anguish. You never quite knew, which Rosa you were to encounter.

As Juan sang, Rosa would hold his hand in hers, for hours. He was Rosa's servant of love. Her state of mind dictated his day. He could be Juan the guitarist, or he could be the consoling companion. Either way Isabella knew their love was as passionate as when they were young.

Leading Rosa to the window, they both stared out at the garden.

"The tree of life." said Rosa in a clear voice and mind. "Ever changing."

Without answering, Juan cradled Rosa in his arms, swaying to a tune he whistled softly. Together they danced, lost in their own world.

Isabella closed the door softly, creeping away so that the lovers could be on their own. Hearing the door close, Rosa took fright.
"Put your hand in mine Rosa. I will never leave your side. There is no need to fear anything. I am with you forever."